Dedication from the Author:

For my parents Bev and Phil

To my dad for inspiring the story
and to my mum for guiding me to write it.

The Fly That Flew

Written by Monique Rowe
Illustrated by Polly Rabbits

MonRowe
BOOKS

The fly that flew, flew **round** and **round**
It flew right **up** and flew back **down**.

It landed on my father's nose
Then flew right **down** and tickled his toes.

My dad he flew **up** from his chair
His paper flew **up** in the air.

He rolled that paper all nice and tight
And swung it around with all his might.

Now the cat, it saw my father's plight
Jumped from its bed and joined in the fight.

It saw the fly and then took chase
The dogs, they thought it was a race.

Under the table
Over the chair

The fly that flew, flew everywhere.
The cat, the dogs, and dad in tow,

There is nowhere that, that fly didn't go.

Around the couch and **through** the door
It is the funniest thing I ever saw.

Down the stairs
And **up** the hall

It drove my father up the wall

13

They went **right** and **left**
And **left** and **right**

Now will they catch it?
Do you think they might?

If you said **NO**!
Then you are ...

From around the corner came my MUM
She flicked open the window with her thumb!

Down the hall and **up** the stairs
Over the table and **under** the chairs

The fly, the cat, the dogs, and dad
They thought they had caught it
They thought they had!

But to their shock
To their dismay
That fly did live to see another day

For through that window
The fly did fly
Through the swings
And into the sky

20

My dad, he sat down in his chair
Unrolled his paper and straightened his hair

But from the corner of it's eye
The cat it saw another fly!

A fly that flew, flew **round** and **round**
It flew right **up** and flew back **down** ......

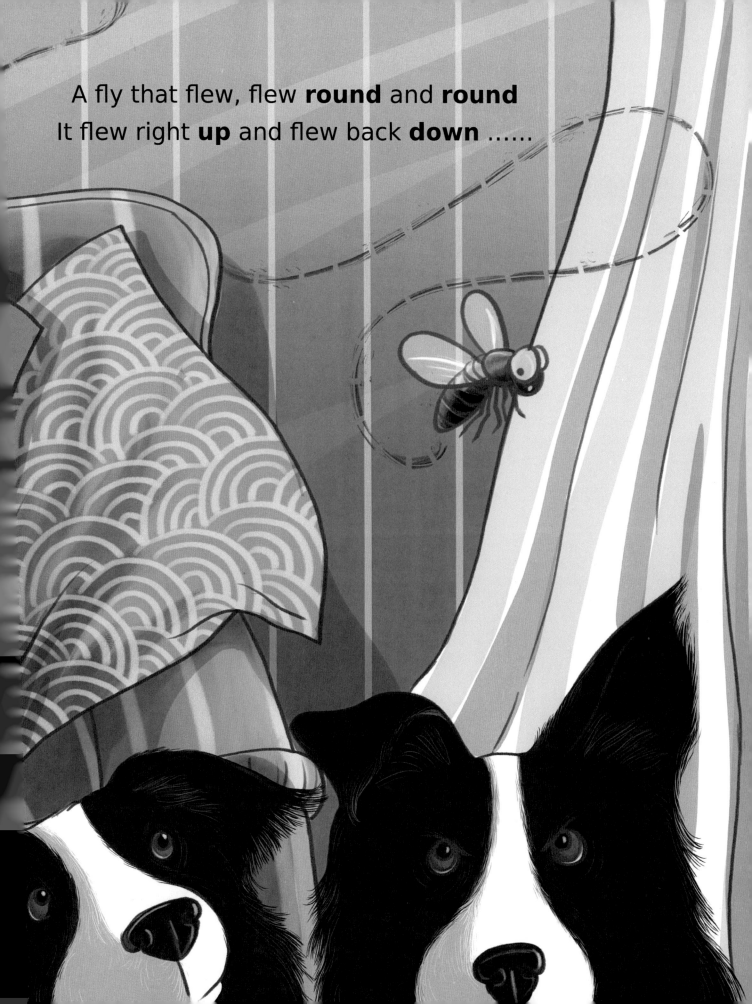

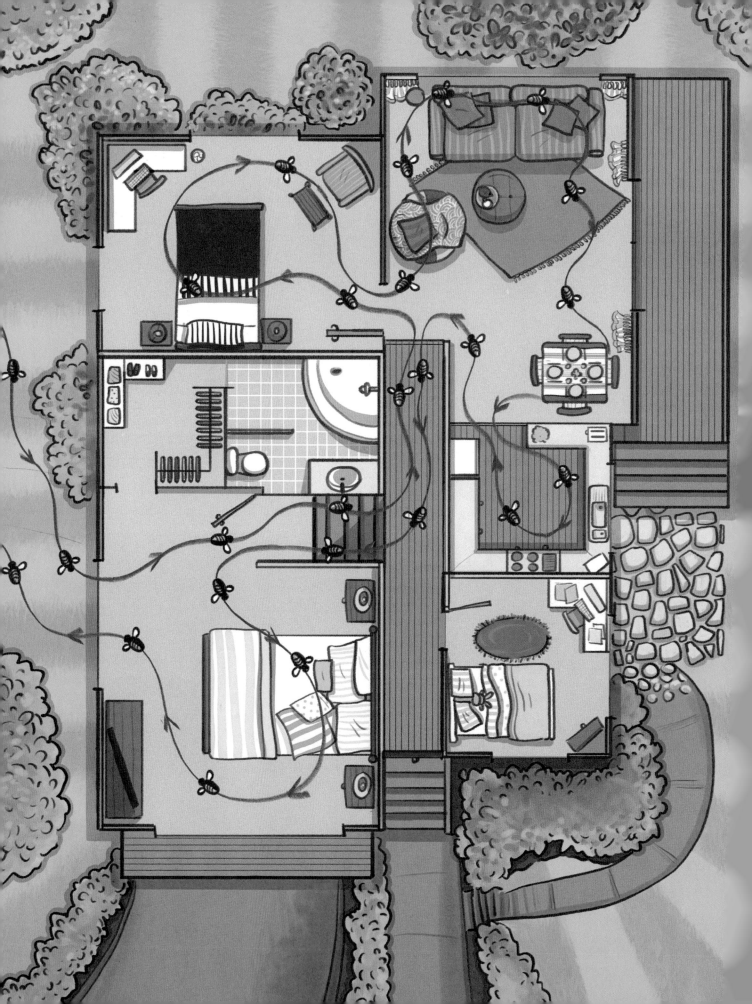

Made in the USA
Las Vegas, NV
28 February 2023

68304631R00017